To my sister Val
RI

To Peter
MK

Rose Impey has become one of Britain's most prominent children's story tellers. She used to be a primary teacher and still spends much of her time working with children.

Moira Kemp is a highly respected illustrator. When illustrating the 'Creepies' she drew heavily from her own childhood experience.

First published in 2004
by Mathew Price Ltd
The Old Glove Factory
Bristol Road, Sherborne
Dorset DT9 4HP

Text copyright © Rose Impey 2001
Illustrations copyright © Moira Kemp 2001

Designed by Douglas Martin
Produced by Mathew Price Ltd
Printed in Singapore

The Midnight Ship

Rose Impey
Illustrated by Moira Kemp

Mathew Price Limited

Sometimes, when visitors come,
I have to sleep with my sister.
Her room's darker
and creepier than mine.

And she always has to have
the top bunk.
"Well, it *is* my bed," she says.
"And *I am the oldest.*"

So I lie there
trying to get to sleep
with her on top
tossing and turning
and the bed rocking
from side to side.

"Keep still!" I whisper,
"You're making me sea-sick."
My sister just giggles
and turns over again.
"It's a bed, not a *boat*," she says.

But later, when Mum's gone downstairs,
and it's all clear,
and the room's getting dark,
my sister whispers to me,
"Come on up! Time to board
The Midnight Ship!"

Then I creep out of bed
and scramble up the ladder
onto the top deck.
Of course, my sister's
already there
steering the ship,
giving the orders,
pretending to be captain.
"Well, it *is* my bed," she says,
"and *I am the oldest*."

But sometimes,
when she's in a good mood,
she lets me steer
while she shines her torch
over the dark blue waves
keeping a look-out
for killer sharks
and deep-sea monsters
and slippery-slimy sea-snakes.

"There's one," she says,
    and I lean over to look.
    But she grabs me by my pyjamas
    and yanks me back.
"Careful you don't fall in," she says,
    and she grins. "They'd eat you alive
    and pick your bones clean
    in minutes."

I screw up my eyes
and peer into the darkness.

"Look! There's one!"
she says. "And another."
But she swings the torch round
too fast for me.
And all I catch is a flash
of their silvery tails
as they disappear
beneath the icy blue water.

I can picture them though:
their heads breaking the waves,
their mouths wide open,
looking for food.
Their poisonous fangs
glistening in the dark.

Suddenly something flies
past my ear.
"Dog overboard!"
cries my sister.

In the torchlight
I can see Danny, her little dog,
bobbing about on the waves.
"Quick!" she says,
and we both race down
to rescue him.

Of course I'm the one
who has to reach out
over the icy cold water
to save him.
"He's your dog," I say.
But she says, "*I am the oldest.*"

So I do it, but I tell her,
"You'd better not let go of me!"
I don't want to end up
splashing about
with sea-snakes all round me.

But suddenly she does
and I land with a . . . bump!

Downstairs a door opens
and our mum shouts up,
"If you two girls
don't stop rocking that bed
there's going to be
real trouble."

We don't need telling twice;
we can tell she means it.
We race back into bed
and we don't make a sound.
We know our mum's still there,
standing in the hall,
listening.

So we lie there in the dark
pretending to be asleep.
But I'm wide awake
watching a finger of light
poking its way
through the curtains
making rippling patterns
on the carpet.

It's *so* quiet now.
I can almost hear the waves
lapping round the legs of my bed.
I can almost see
the slippery sea-snakes
wriggling and writhing
in the water beneath me.

It's all right for my sister,
up there, out of reach.
But I'm down here
just above them
and I start to think how easily
they could get me,
coiling themselves
up the legs of the bed.
Any minute now
they could slide and slither
under the end of my quilt.

Ugh! I start to shiver
and I snuggle down the bed.
But my foot touches something
cold . . . and slippery.
I snatch it away
as if I've had an electric shock.

"S-S-Sarah!" I whisper.
But there's no answer.

I can't believe it!
She's gone to sleep
and left me
all on my own
in the dark.
I tell myself,
there's nothing there,
nothing at all.
I probably imagined it.
And I slide my foot down
one more time,
just to be sure.

Aaaah! I feel it again.
Cold and smooth.
And this time I know
there's a slippery sea-snake
about to wrap itself
around my ankles.
Any moment it will sink
its poisonous fangs
into my legs.
It will eat me alive!
It will pick my bones clean!

I try to scream,
but no sound
comes out at all.
He-e-elp! He-e-elp!

I kick
and kick
and kick
until my quilt flies up in the air.

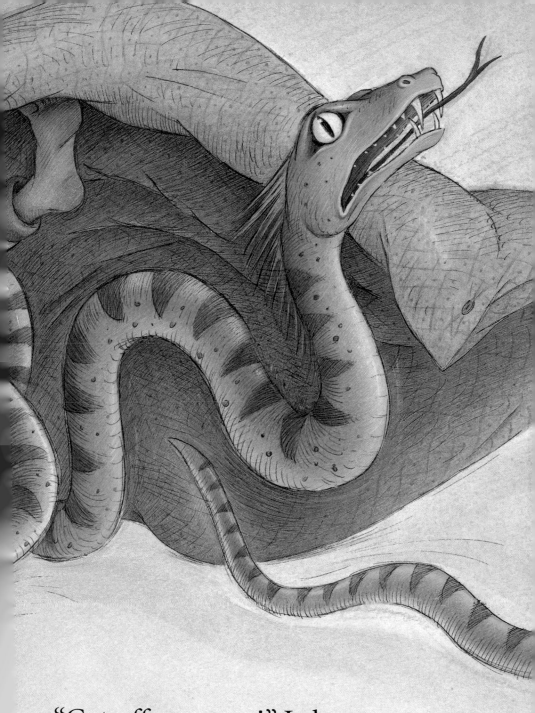

"Get off meeeeee!" I shout.

There's a loud BANG!
as *something* lands
on the floor.

The hall door opens again
and footsteps come
running upstairs.
Now we're in trouble.

"What's all this noise?"
says Mum. "And what's that
doing there?" It's my sister's torch
lying in the middle of the carpet.

"I thought it was a slippery sea-snake,"
 I say, "coming to eat me alive."
 My mum shakes her head
 and looks at my sister.
"I wonder where she could
 have got that silly idea from?" she says.
 My sister grins. "She probably
 read it in some stupid book."

But my mum knows
better than that.
She gives my sister
a bit of a telling-off.
After all, she says,
She is the oldest.